The Chronicles of California's Queen Calafia

RETOLD FROM
Garci Rodriguez de Montalvo's
1587 Castilian Edition of Amadis, Book 5,
The Adventures of Esplandian, Chapter 157
Illustrated with Woodcuts from
French Editions of Amadis de Gaule,
Published between 1548 and 1555

SELECTION AND INTRODUCTION
Mozelle Sukut, Ph.D.

TRANSLATION
Constance Kihyet, Ph.D.

DESIGN
Felicia O'Beirne

Trails of Discovery
Publishers © 2007

THE CHRONICLES OF CALIFORNIA'S QUEEN CALAFIA
Mozelle Sukut

Copyright © 2007 by Trails of Discovery
All rights reserved. No reproduction of this book in whole or part or stored in or introduced into a retrieval system, or transmitted, in any form, electronic, mechanical, photocopying, recording or otherwise, may be made without written authorization of the copyright publisher.

Trails of Discovery
31071 Marbella Vista
San Juan Capistrano, CA 92675

First edition
ISBN: 978-0-9788926-0-9
1. Fiction - Spanish translation into English
2. Amazons

Printed in the USA.

Contents

IMAGE CREDITS	4
PREFACE	5
INTRODUCTION	6
LAS SERGAS DE ESPLANDIAN, CHAPTER 157 *By Garci Rodriguez de Montalvo, 1587 edition* Modern English translation of the Castilian Spanish	17
HISTORICAL CHRONOLOGY	74
FURTHER READING	75
PUBLIC ART DEPICTING MONTALVO'S QUEEN CALAFIA	76

Image Credits

The woodcuts in this volume are reproduced from rare sixteenth century French folio editions of Amadis de Gaule, published by Vincent Serlenas and others, and produced between 1548 and 1555. Images from the 1548 and 1550 editions are reproduced with the very kind permission of the Folger Shakespeare Library in Washington, D.C. Amadis de Gaule, PQ6275F21, volumes 1-4: Woman with lion - volume 3, book 9, chapter XXXV, sig. P6, Veil. LXXXVIII; Dragon ship - volume 2, book 5, chapter XXXLLL, sig. L5v; King on horse with knight fighting lion - volume 1, book 1, chapter I, sig. A1r, fueillet I; Women on horseback - volume 1, book 1, chapter XXXV, sig. V3r, Fueillet CXVII; Knight and lady meeting on horses - volume 1, book 1, chapter VI, sig. Dor, Fueillet XOX; Battle scene - volume 3, book 9, chapter XLVI, sig. O2v, Fueil. LXXXv; Queen with knights - volume 3, book 9, chapter XL, sig. R4v, Feil.XCVLLLv; Figures standing around table - volume 2, book 6, chapter XXXVL, sig. O2v, Fueil. LXXXv; Two couples - volume 1, book 1, chapter ll, sig. Aiiii, fueillet LLLL.

The Amazon figure is from the 1611 edition of Iconologia by Cesare Ripa, courtesy of The Bancroft Library, University of California, Berkeley.

Preface

After several years of unsuccessfully searching for a copy of California's oldest tale about the mythical Queen Calafia and her island, I became even more determined to locate one. Where were original or later editions? Were there illustrations or woodcuts produced for the fable? The quest took several turns to locate any editions of the original by the Spanish author, Garci Rodriguez de Montalvo, in his novel titled "Las Sergas de Esplandian", written during the first decade of the 16th century. I was fortunate to purchase one of E.E. Hales' 1945 limited editions of "The Queen of California" which had been first published in 1864 in the Atlantic Monthly magazine. In it he stated his belief that California had been named by Spanish conquistadors for the mythical island in Montalvo's fable. I also located a readable reprint of the 1587 Castilian edition in Madrid. An original 1555 French edition became available from a book shop in London in remarkable condition with many illustrations within the text. Locating additional woodcuts was a challenge, but some were discovered in early French editions of Amadis de Gaule, safely held in rare book sections of several major libraries. The pursuit of these old volumes has resulted in learning about the time in which Montalvo wrote the adventures of his book's main hero, Amadis. The medieval setting of the last decade of the 15th century was one of Christian knights' determination to clear the Iberian peninsula of Moors. Montalvo lived and wrote during these turbulent times in Medino del Campo in Castile, in the middle of the amazing mixture of cultures which interacted there and had tolerated each other for the decades before.

My thanks to Dr. Constance Kihyet for translating the old Castilian Spanish, to the Folger Library for the use of their rare woodcuts from their 16th century French folio editions of Amadis de Gaule, and to Felicia O'Beirne for the visual appeal of this edition.

Introduction

long the Pyrenees then south through Old and New Castile and down to Andalusia from 750 AD to 1500, violent battles between Muslim and Christian armies produced legendary as well as historical material which became the medieval literature of the 15th and 16th centuries. For eight hundred years the Moors had dominated the area we know today as Spain. For short periods, especially when the Andalusian culture was at its peak, many Christians, Muslims and Jews lived and worked together in tolerance of each other's beliefs and traditions. The final end of this tolerance began in 1480 with the Inquisition and crescendoed in 1492 with the overthrow of Granada. By the mid-15th century the Moors had been pushed into southern Granada, and Christian Spain had organized into three kingdoms (Portugal, Castile/ Leon, and Aragon). Christians were determined to take all of the peninsula, and crusading enthusiasm was at a peak from 1481 to 1492, the period of war against Granada. The only proper activity then for a man was to fight, and 16th century Spanish soldiers were the best in the world. Even volunteers from the rest of Europe came, spurred by religious belief and the romance of chivalry. Historians describe a tournament atmosphere during the Granada siege with the Moors and Christian knights occasionally engaging in chivalrous combat.

Miniature from the Toledan School of Alfonso X, Muslim and Christian knights embracing in greeting.

With the atmosphere of the times still dominated by crusading fervor after Granada was overtaken, but with no more Moors or Jews to kill, the lure of new worlds became the talk of Spain—gold, spices, exotic people and lands to plunder. Starting with Columbus, who gave his discovered lands to Castile, followed by Amerigo Vespuccis' voyages, then Cortez and others, the explorers of the New World returned home first to the Atlantic ports of Spain's coast. The whole of Spain was alive with stories of these first voyages to the New World. To the north, Medina del Campo was the financial and commercial center of Castile and the major crossroad of cultures, where merchants' goods from all over Western Europe were housed and traded. Medina del Campo had also been the center of the battlegrounds where the Moors and Christians fought for supremacy of Spain in the 10th and 11th centuries. The town's Moorish fortress passed to Ferdinand and Isabella after their marriage which united the areas of Castile and Aragon. In 1492, two different events were set in motion in Medina del Campo: Columbus solicited the backing of Isabella for the exploration of new worlds, and Garci Rodriguez de Montalvo, a veteran and regidor (city councilor) who lived there, was creating what was to become one of the most widely read novels of the next century.

Map of medieval Spain.

pic battles of decades past and fantasy locales of the New World became the stuff of the knight fairy tale romances of chivalry. These tales were the favorite reading of medieval Christians. In the major countries of Europe, the adventure books of Montalvo were among the most widely read and influential secular works of the 16th century. They were read as entertainment, as books of war, morals and virtue. Battles and beasts, eroticism and heroic feats, humor and the arts of proper conversation and diplomacy were all included. These incredible adventures fed the enthusiasm of knights and navigators who were learning about the distant unexplored world of America. Rumors about these lands included myths of wealthy islands, amazing beasts and beautiful Amazons, just as they were written about in the knight's adventure tales. The first Spanish conquistadores to explore America were among their most ardent readers. And most widely read was Montalvo's Book 5, Las Sergas de Esplandian, which included a chapter about an Amazon queen who ruled a mythical island called California.

Iconologia

The Amazon figure was used as an emblem for the new world. This image from the 1611 edition of Iconologia, by Cesare Ripa, courtesy of the Bancroft Library, University of California, Berkeley.

In his chapter about Calafia, Montalvo used the battle over Constantinople as his setting. When he was a youth in 1453, the Christians had lost Constantinople to the Moors, but in his fable, he created intrigue, chivalry and a different outcome. He wrote that the old hero, King Amadis, journeyed to Constantinople to defend it against Pagans, and he created the King's son, a strong and handsome knight, Esplandian. To add further excitement, Montalvo created a spectacular island called California, full of gold and inhabited by mythical beasts and beautiful Amazons. In most knights' tales, there was primarily nobility and male dominance, but Montalvo created a heroine with an agenda who could change her mind, influence her troops and command secret weapons. Conquistadores reached the Pacific in the 1520s, and Hernando Cortez or others named the land along the Pacific coast California in the 1540s, perhaps because it reminded the explorers of the enchanted island in Montalvo's popular tale. This connection was not recognized by scholars until 1862, when Edward Hale stumbled across Montalvo's ancient book.

Comme le Roy Amadis & son filz Espládian comba=
tirent le Soudan de Lique & la Royne Calafie, &
de la bataille qui fut le iour mesmes par mer & par
terre, entre les Chrestiens & Payens.

Chapitre   LIII.

FROM AMADIS DE GAULE, BOOK 5, 1555 EDITION.

he first printed edition of Amadis de Gaule was published by Montalvo in 1508 in the town of Zaragoz. The art of printing had arrived early in Spain, in the 1470s. From around 1490 to 1500, Montalvo rewrote the romance adventures of the knight King Amadis originally written in the previous decades by another writer (probably French or Portuguese) into three books, giving those 14th century manuscripts their shape known today. Wanting to write a glorious tale himself, he composed Book 4, first known printing in 1508, and Book 5, the first known printing in 1510, which contains his Calafia chapter. His own tales in Book 4 and 5 were probably conceived and written in the 1490s but no earlier editions have been found. In England and Germany, Amadis was widely known through its French translations by Nicolas de Herberay des Essarts. Montalvo's Books 1 through 5 went on to have numerous publications during the next 150 years.

From the first edition of
Amadis de Gaula, Book 1, 1508.

LIBRO PRIMERO
DE LAS SERGAS DEL MVY ESFORÇADO
CAVALLERO ESPLANDIAN;
hijo del excelente Rey Amadis de Gaula.

AORA NVEVA MENTE EMENDADAS EN ESTA
Impression, de muchos errores que en las Impressiones passadas auia.

EN BVRGOS.

Impresso con licencia, en casa de Simon de Aguaya.
Anno M.D. LX XX VI I.

Title page from the 1587 edition of
Las Sergas de Esplandian.

LAS SERGAS DE ESPLANDIAN, CHAPTER 157
BY GARCI RODRIGUEZ DE MONTALVO

An Island Called California

Now you are going to hear the most extraordinary tale that was ever heralded in any chronicles, or ever in the memory of mankind, in which the great city of Constantinople was engaged in combat and would have been conquered on the following day of battle; yet when confronted with danger, the defending forces rallied. Know then, that due east of the Indies there is an island called California, very near to the locale called the Terrestrial Paradise. It was populated by black women, with no men among them, for they lived in the fashion of Amazons. They possessed strong and firm bodies of ardent courage and great strength. Their island was the strongest in all the world, with steep cliffs and rocky shores. Their arms were decorated with gold, as were the harnesses of the wild beasts they tamed and rode. Throughout the whole island there was no other metal but gold. Their dwellings were caves wrought out of island rock with great labor. They had a fleet of ships with which they sailed out to loot other locales in order to obtain bountiful treasures.

Gryphon illustrated by Albrecht Durer, 1515.

Creatures of California

n this island called California there were found many creatures known as griffins, which had never before been seen in any other part of the world, because the vast ruggedness of the terrain hosted an infinite number of these wild beasts. When these griffins were still small creatures, the women set traps to capture them. Covering themselves with very thick animal hides, the women captured the young griffins, which they took to their rocky caves where they nurtured and raised them. Being themselves quite a match for the griffins, the island women fed them with men they had taken as prisoners and with male children to whom they had given birth. They brought up the creatures with such care that they in turn received many benefits from the griffins which never caused them harm or injury. Every man who landed on the shores of the island was immediately devoured by these creatures. Even when they were no longer hungry, the griffins would seize men as prey in their mighty claws, carrying them high above the earth and then dropping them to their deaths below.

From Amadis de Gaula, Book 9, 1548 edition.

Queen Calafia

As you will recall from historical records, during the days when mighty Pagan warriors sailed with great fleets to distant shores of the world, there reigned in the island of California a mighty and beautiful queen. She was more ambitious, daring and courageous than any of the rulers who had previously occupied the throne. She was aware that the greater part of the world around her island was waging war in a great onslaught against Christian forces. She knew virtually nothing about them, as she had been isolated from other civilizations outside her realm. Aware of her rank and prowess as the leader of a powerful female army, she desired to explore the world and capture bountiful treasures, just like many great princes and lords who had embarked on similar expeditions. So she began to engage in talks with those most skilled in warfare and to seek their advice in the art of military strategy. Her ambitious nature and references to the great profits and honors to be gained in such enterprise excited all those with whom she consulted. Above all, the Queen focused on the great worldwide fame that was to be gained in such heroic battle. She noted that if the island women remained secluded as their grandmothers had done before them, they would in essence be buried alive, doomed to passing their days without hope of fame or glory, just as beasts of burden.

From Amadis de Gaule, Book 5, 1550 edition.

California's Great Fleet Made Ready

So powerful was the moving speech of this mighty queen, known as Calafia to her island subjects, that they were not only moved to consent wholeheartedly to this enterprise, but also begged her to hasten to sea so that they might readily earn these honors in alliance with great male warriors. The Queen, noting the eagerness of her subjects, immediately gave orders to stock her great fleet with all the essential foods and armor of gold necessary for the journey. Then she commanded that her largest sailing vessel should be prepared and secured with bars of the strongest timber in which were placed more than five hundred griffins which you recall had been trained since birth to feed on men. In addition, she ordered that the wild beasts on which she and her subjects rode should be boarded for the voyage, along with the most skillful warriors of her island. Then, after taking measures to secure the island kingdom during her absence, the Queen and her armed fleet set sail.

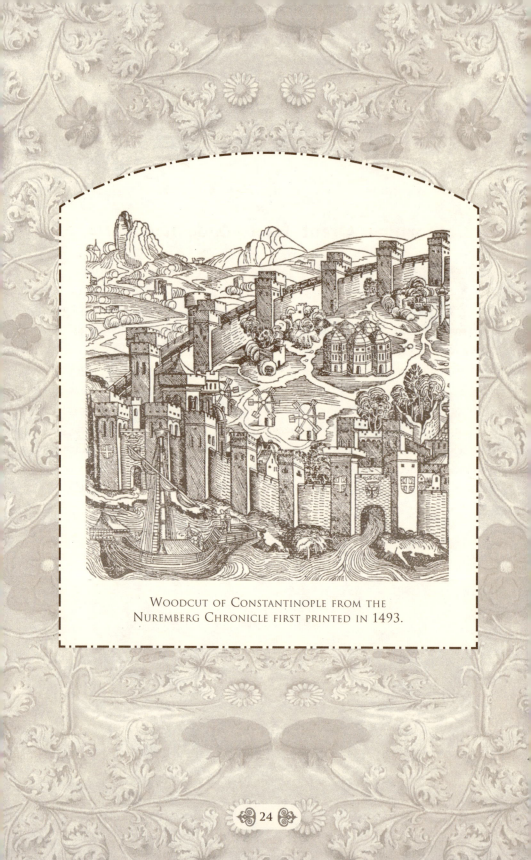

Woodcut of Constantinople from the Nuremberg Chronicle first printed in 1493.

The Women Warriors Arrive in Constantinople

he fleet made such haste that they joined the fleets of the Pagan warriors after the battle I have just described to you, so that they were received with great joy. The fleet was visited at once by many great lords, who welcomed them with jubilation. Because she wished to know all about the current state of affairs on the battle scene, the Queen asked the leaders many questions, which they answered completely. Then she remarked, "You have fought this city with your great forces and you have not been able to conquer it. Now, if you are willing, I wish to see what my forces can accomplish tomorrow, provided you will give orders accordingly." All the great lords replied they would give this command as she requested. "Then send instructions to all your other captains that tomorrow neither they nor their forces should leave their camps until I command them, and you shall witness a battle more remarkable than you have ever seen or heard of before." Word was sent immediately to the great Sultan of Liquia, and the Sultan of Halapa, who commanded all the forces stationed there. They in turn gave these same orders to their warriors, who were left to wonder about the thinking of this queen.

From Amadis de Gaule, Book 5, 1555 edition.

The Griffins Attack the Christian Knights

hen night ended and morning broke, Queen Calafia went on shore with her army of women, all outfitted with their armor of gold and adorned with the most precious stones, which were abundant on the island of California, like stones in the field. The women mounted their fierce beasts, richly draped as I have told you. Then she ordered that the ship's door to the griffins' cage should be opened. When the creatures saw the fields before them, they rushed with great haste, gleefully flying and immediately catching sight of the group of men close by. Since they were famished and fearless, every griffin pounced upon a man, seized him in his claws and carried him high into the air and began to devour his prey. Although the onlookers shot them with many arrows and gave them many strong blows with lances and swords, the creatures' tight feathers protected them, so that no one could strike through to their flesh. For their army, this was the loveliest agreeable chase ever seen. As the Pagans saw them flying on high with their enemies, they unleashed loud clear cries of joy that pierced the heavens. But for those in the city, it was the saddest and most bitter scene, when fathers saw their sons lifted in the air and brothers witnessed the same fate of their brothers. They all wept and screamed, and it was a sorrowful sight indeed. When the griffins had flown for some time and had dropped their prized catches on the earth and sea, they turned sharply and fearlessly as they did upon their arrival and seized many more helpless victims, bringing great joy to their masters and great misery to the Christians. The terror was so great among the onlookers that some took refuge by hiding under the vaults of the city towers, while others disappeared from the ramparts, leaving no forces for their defense. Seeing this, Queen Calafia loudly commanded the two Sultans in charge of the troops to send for the ladders, for the city had been conquered. At once they rushed forward, positioned their ladders and mounted the city walls.

From Amadis de Gaule, Book 1, 1548 edition.

The Griffins Attack the Pagan Knights

Meanwhile the griffins, having abandoned their previous victims, eyed the Pagans of whom they had no prior knowledge, and seized them just as they had seized Christians. Then flying through the air, they carried them up and allowed them to plunge to their deaths, permitting none to escape mortal injury. Thus was exchanged the pleasure for pain of battle. For those on the outside now were those who were mourning with great sorrow the loss of those who had been so brutally handled. Those who were within, who had believed themselves defeated by the enemy, now took great comfort. At this moment, those on the ramparts stopped, stricken with panic, fearing they would die in the same way of their comrades. Simultaneously the Christians leaped from their hiding places in the vaults and quickly slew many Turks who had gathered on the walls while compelling others to leap down. They sprang back to their secure hiding places when they saw the griffins returning. Upon seeing the toll of the battle, Queen Calafia sadly remarked, "O ye idols in whom I believe and worship, what is this which has happened as favorably to my friends as to my enemies? I believed with your aid and my strong forces and great weapons I should be able to destroy them. But it has not proved to be so."

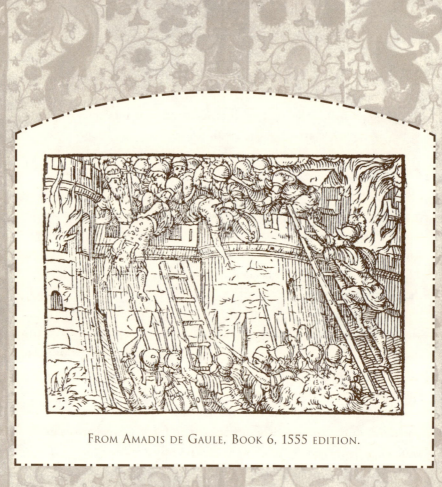

From Amadis de Gaule, Book 6, 1555 edition.

Mounting the Ladders

hen she ordered her women warriors to mount the ladders to try to gain the towers and draw their swords on those who took refuge there from the griffins. They obeyed the Queen's commands, dismounted and placed over their breasts breastplates that no weapon could pierce, and as I previously told you, with armor of gold to protect their legs and arms. Quickly they crossed the plain and mounted the ladders steadily and invaded the whole circuit of the city walls, and thus began to battle fiercely with those who had taken refuge in the vaults of the towers. They defended themselves bravely but found themselves surrounded within quarters that were well protected by narrow doors. Those of the city who remained in the streets below shot arrows and darts at the women, piercing them through the sides, so that they received many wounds because their golden armor was weak there. Then the griffins returned, soaring above them and refusing to leave them.

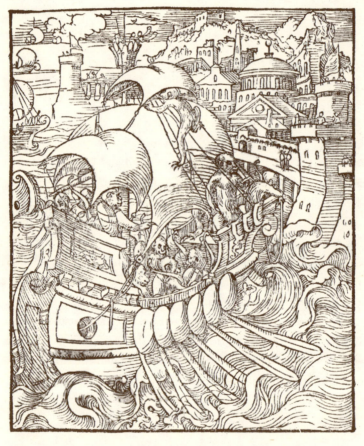

From Amadis de Gaule, Book 5, 1555 edition.

The Griffins Are Recalled

hen Queen Calafia saw this, she cried out to the Sultans, "Order your troops to mount so they can defend my forces against those brutes who dare attack them."

At once the Sultans commanded their troops to ascend the ladders and gain the circle and the surrounding towers so that by nightfall the entire army might rejoin them in their plan to conquer the city. The soldiers rushed from their camps and mounted the walls where the women were engaged in battle. But when the griffins saw them approach, they seized them ravenously, as if they had not caught any prey that day. When the women threatened them with knives, they became only more enraged, so although the knights took shelter for themselves, the griffins dragged them out with force, lifted them up into the air and then let them fall to their deaths. The fear and panic of the Pagans was so great that, with more haste than they had mounted the walls, did they climb down to take refuge in their camp. The Queen, seeing this plan falling apart, immediately ordered those who had guarded the griffins to recall them and enclose them up in the ship. Upon hearing the Queen's command, they mounted on top of the ship's mast, and called out loudly to the griffins in their vernacular tongue. Consequently, they all obeyed and returned obediently to their cages, as if they were humans called to order.

From Amadis de Gaule, Book 5, 1555 edition.*

The Battle Resumes on City Walls

The Sultans may certainly have doubted whether their new alliance with Queen Calafia was what they had hoped it would be. She felt this herself, and remarked to them: "Since my arrival has caused you so much injury, I wish that it may bring you an equal amount of pleasure. Command your troops to come out and we will approach the city against those knights who dare to challenge us. Then we will engage them in the most severe combat in which my troops and I will position ourselves at the front of battle." The Sultans then ordered their armored warriors to rush immediately to join in mounting the rampart, now that the griffins were secured away from the scene. With the horsemen following Queen Calafia closely, the army rushed and pressed upon the wall, although not as successfully as they had expected, because the townspeople were already positioned there prepared to fight. As the Pagan forces mounted upon their ladders, the Christian forces threw them backwards resulting in injury and death to many. Others pressed forward with iron picks and other tools, and dug fiercely into a circuit of the wall. The wall structure was already distressed and weakened by oils and other things hurled upon them, but not enough that they succeeded in making many gaps and openings. When news of this approach reached the Emperor of Constantinople, who kept ten thousand horsemen ready at his command, he ordered them all to defend those weakened places as best they could. To the dismay and grief of the Pagans, the townspeople repaired the openings with timbers, stones and mounds of earth.

From Amadis de Gaule, Book 5, 1555 edition.

The Fierce Battle at the Aquilena Gate

hen the Queen saw this resistance, she quickly rushed with her attendants to the Aquilena gate, which was guarded by Norandel, half-brother of Amadis and another son of Lisuarte, King of England. She went in advance of the others, wholly covered with one of those shields which we have described before, and with her lance held firmly in her hand. Upon seeing her approach, Norandel went to meet her, and they clashed so vehemently that their lances were broken into pieces, yet neither of them fell to the ground. Norandel quickly put his hand on his sword, and the Queen put her hand on her great knife with a blade wider than a palm frond. They began to strike one another with blow after blow. At once others joined in a melee, one against the other, all so dazzled and confused by such terrible blows that it was a great marvel to behold. Just when some of the female warriors fell to the ground, so did some of the cavaliers fall to the earth. If this history does not convey the details of this forceful battle and the courage of the combatants, it is because there were such great numbers that fell so quickly on one another that even Great Master Helisabat who witnessed the scene could not begin to describe the fiercest battle you have ever heard of. The tumult was so great that once the battle between these two was finished, those on each side ran to the aid of their chief.

From Amadis de Gaule, Book 5, 1555 edition.

Calafia's Excellence in Battle

ow I must tell you that the things this queen did in battle, such as the slaying of knights and throwing them wounded from their mounts; these were such feats that it is hard to describe or believe that a female warrior has ever demonstrated such great prowess. As she dealt with so many noble knights, not one of them let her escape without striking her many heavy blows, which she received upon her very strong hard shield. When Talaque and Maneli, the Kings of Ireland, saw what the Queen was doing in battle and the great losses their troops suffered by her hands, they rushed out striking her with blows, as if they considered her possessed. Meanwhile the Queen's sister Liota, who witnessed their attack, rushed in like a mad lioness to relieve her, and pressed the knights so mortally that she rescued Calafia from their power and placed her among her own troops again. At this stage of the battle, you might say the people of the fleets had taken the advantage, and had it not been for the mercy of God and the great force of Count Frandalo and his companions, the city would have been completely lost to the enemy. Many fell dead on both sides, with many more of the Pagan forces falling because they wore the weaker armor.

From Amadis de Gaule, Book 1, 1548 edition.

Fighting Ceases for the Night

As you have heard, this fierce and cruel battle continued nearly until nightfall. At this time there were no open gates, except the one guarded by Norandel. The knights had been withdrawn from the others and should have bolted them, but the truth was very different, as I will explain. For as the two Sultans greatly desired to see Calafia's warriors engage in battle, they had forbidden their own people to enter into combat. But when they saw the day's events unfolding, they pushed against the Christians so fiercely that they might all enter the city. More than a hundred men and women did enter there. And the Emperor of Constantinople, guided by God who directed him to keep the other gates closed, knowing in what direction the battle was going, pressed them so hard with his knights that he drove some out, while killing some as well. Then the Pagans suffered many losses as they were killed from the watchtowers. More than two hundred women warriors were slain. Those within were not without great loss, for ten of the crusaders were killed, bringing great sorrow to their companions. They were Ledaderin de Fajarque, Trion and Imosil de Borgona, and the two sons of Isanjo. All of the people of the city returned, and the Pagan forces also returned to their camps. Queen Calafia rejoined her fleet because she had not taken quarters on shore. The other combatants boarded their own ships, so there was no further fighting that day. Meanwhile, Amadis, King of Gaul and father of Esplandian, arrived at Constantinople.

Illustration in incunabula (from books printed before 1501), reproduced from Der Bilderschmuck der Fruhdrucke, Leipzig, 1920.

A Challenge to King Amadis and his Son Esplandian is Issued by Sultan Radiaro and Queen Calafia

e, Radiaro Sultan of Liquia, shield and rampart of Pagan Law, destroyer of Christians, cruel enemy of the Gods, and the most mighty Queen Calafia, Lady of the great island of California, famous for its abundance of gold and precious stones, announce to you, Amadis of Gaul, King of Great Britain, and your son Esplandian, Knight of the Great Serpent, that we have come here with the intention of destroying the city of Constantinople, because of the injury and loss which the honored King Amato of Persia, our cousin and friend, has received from this evil Emperor, who has fraudulently taken part of his territory. We also desire to gain more glory and fame in this contest, as fortune has already bestowed on us, for we are aware of your great chivalric reputation throughout the world. We have agreed, and propose to you, that our forces should engage in battle in the presence of this great gathering of nations, and at the end of the conflict, the conquered should submit to the will of the conqueror, or retreat to the place they are ordered to go. If you refuse this proposition, we shall join all your past triumphs to our history, counting them as glories of our own, and the future will record the victory as ours.

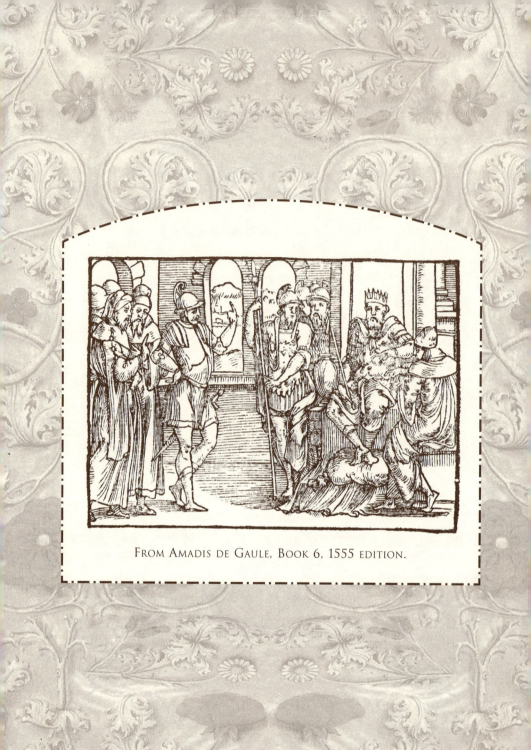

From Amadis de Gaule, Book 6, 1555 edition.

The Challenge is Delivered to the Christian Camp by Queen Calafia's Messenger and the Rules of Combat Are Proposed

ing Amadis: "My good lords, as the affairs of men and nations are in the hands and will of God from which no one can escape, if we withdraw from their demand for battle, it would only encourage our enemies and injure our honor, especially here in this distant land of strangers where our well-known worldly power has not yet been tested. Although we may be regarded as courageous in our homeland, nevertheless here we would be judged as great cowards. Therefore placing confidence in the Lord's mercy, I have decided that the battle shall take place immediately." "If you wish this," replied King Lisuarte and King Perion, "we accept the challenge and may God help you with His grace!" Then King Amadis said to the female messenger, "Friend, inform your lord and Queen Calafia that we wish to battle with those weapons of their choosing; the battle will take place on this field, which shall be divided down the middle. I promise that whatever happens, our other forces will not rescue us from danger. Let them give the same order to their forces, and if they wish to begin combat now, now it shall be." The damsel departed with the King's reply, which she delivered to the two princes.

Parchment manuscript which belonged to Queen Isabella, 14th century, El Escorial Library, Madrid.

Queen Calafia Wishes to See Esplandian

ueen Calafia questioned the messenger about the appearance of the Christians. "They are very noble, for they are handsome and well-equipped knights. But I tell you, Queen, that among them, the Knight of the Serpent, Esplandian, son of Amadis, is unlike any prince of the past, present or even future. I have never seen, nor will ever see, such a handsome elegant prince. Oh Queen, what can I say except if he were of our same faith, we might believe our Gods made him with their own hands, with all their power and wisdom, for he lacks nothing." Upon hearing this, the Queen replied, "Damsel, my friend, your words exaggerate." "No," she replied, "Unless you see him yourself, there is no other way to know of his great excellence." "Then I say," said the Queen, "I will not engage in battle with such a man until I have first seen and spoken with him. I request that the Sultan arrange for us to meet." The Sultan did agree. Turning on her horse, the damsel approached the camp again. All thought that she had brought the terms of agreement for the impending combat. As she approached, she called the waiting Kings to the tent door, saying, "King Amadis, Queen Calafia demands that you assure her of a safe meeting tomorrow with your son." Amadis laughed and said to the Kings, "What do you think of this demand?" "Let her come," replied King Lisuarte. "It will be a very good thing to see the most distinguished woman in the world." "Then take this for your reply," said Amadis to the damsel, "say that she will be treated truthfully and honorably." The damsel received this message and delivered it to the Queen who in turn told Sultan Radiaro, "Wait until I have seen him in person, and instruct your forces to hold off, so there is no battle until then." "Of this you may be certain," he said.

From Amadis de Gaule, Book 5, 1555 edition.

Queen Calafia Prepares to Meet Esplandian

alafia immediately returned to her fleet where she pondered throughout the night whether or not she should take weapons to the meeting. Finally she decided a more dignified approach would be to dress in feminine attire. When she awakened the next day, she directed her people to bring one of her golden dresses encrusted with many precious stones as well as her artfully crafted turban. The voluminous headdress had abundant fabric, and she wore it like a hood. It was made completely of gold, embroidered with valuable stones. Then they brought out a strange animal for her to ride, the most peculiar beast ever seen, for it had ears as large as two shields, a broad forehead centered by a single eye that shined like a mirror, and large nostrils on its short, blunt nose. From its mouth protruded two tusks, each the length of two palms. Its yellow skin displayed many violet spots like a leopard. It was larger than a dromedary, had feet cleft like an ox, yet it could run swiftly as the wind and skip over the rocks holding itself upright like a mountain goat. Its diet consisted only of dates, figs and peas. Its thighs, hips and breast were very beautiful. On such an exotic animal mounted the beautifully dressed Queen, followed by two thousand women of her entourage, adorned in the richest finery. Another twenty damsels brought up the rear of the procession, each dressed in uniform, with lengthy trains of their dresses draping the beasts they rode, dragging some four fathoms behind. With such equipment and ornament the Queen proceeded to the Emperor's camp, where the Kings awaited her arrival on the plain. They were seated on richly decorated chairs upholstered in golden cloth. Since they did not have much faith in the promise of the Pagan warriors, they were bearing arms. They came out to receive her at the tent door where she dismounted from her beast into the arms of Don Quadragente, a noted giant previously conquered by Amadis and now the King's ally. Both King Lisuarte and Perion took her by the hands and seated her in a chair between them.

From an Italian manuscript of the Grail Quest, c. 1400.

Queen Calafia Meets Esplandian

She could now see Esplandian next to King Lisuarte, who held him by the hand. She immediately recognized the famous knight from the superiority of his good looks, and thought to herself, "Oh my Gods! What is this? I proclaim I have never seen anyone who can be compared to him nor shall I ever see any like him again." When he turned his beautiful eyes on her lovely face, the bright rays of his resplendent beauty heated her heart with amorous passion, as if she had been wielded between mallets of iron. With this vision, the Queen felt that if she stayed any longer, her great fame which had been won by many daring knightly actions might be jeopardized. If she delayed, she risked exposing herself to the dishonor of submitting to the wiles of her feminine softness, and therefore painfully resisted the feelings she had subjected to her free will. Rising from her seat, she announced, "Knight of the Great Serpent, I have made inquiry about the two standards of excellence which distinguish you above all other mortals. First, the excellence of your legendary handsome looks, which one must see to describe. And second, your valor and strength of your brave heart. The first I have observed to be so great that I could never again see it surpassed even if granted years of searching. The other, your mighty bravery, will be seen on the battlefield against the brave Radiaro, Sultan of Liquia. My courage shall be tested against the mighty King Amadis, your father. If fortune should grant that we survive this battle, as well as those to be fought in the future, then I will address you with some of my own affairs before I return to my home."

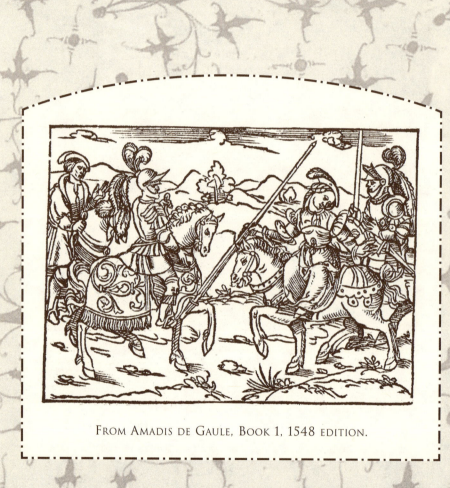

From Amadis de Gaule, Book 1, 1548 edition.

The Queen Departs to Prepare for Combat

Then she turned toward the Kings and addressed them, "Kings, rest in good health. I now return to dress for the battlefield differently from this, hoping that on that field King Amadis, who entrusts his victory to the fate in fickle fortune that he would never be conquered by a brave knight or frightening beasts, but will be by a woman." Taking the two older Kings by the hand, she bade them farewell and allowed them to help her mount upon her strange steed. Esplandian made no gesture or salute whatsoever as she departed. He made no reply in part because he regarded her as something both strange yet beautiful, and because he saw her come bearing arms, which was so different from the way a woman should have arrived to a meeting of kings. He considered it dishonorable that this queen would stray from God's commandment that women should be in subjection to men, but should instead prefer to be the dominant ruler of men by force and battle. Most importantly, he hated to place himself in any relationship with her because she was one of the despised infidels he had vowed to destroy at all costs.

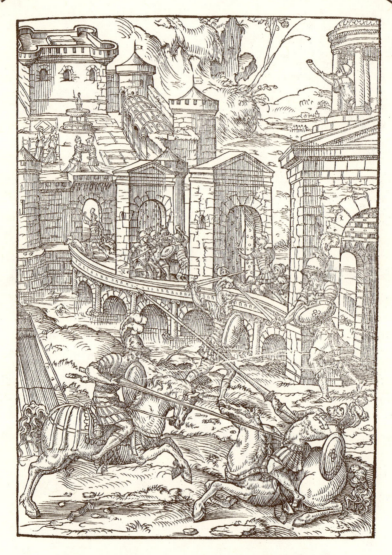

From Amadis De Gaule, Book 9, 1548 edition.

The Celebrated Encounter of the Four Heroes

attle preparations were made, and the combat rules were set. They separated for a while and then rode furiously at each other at full speed. The Sultan struck Esplandian on the shield with such a hard blow that part of the lance pierced it deeply, leaving witnesses to believe it had passed through his body, although this was not so. The lance passed beneath his arm without touching him. Esplandian, knowing his beloved lady, Princess Leonorina, the Emperor of Constantinople's daughter, was watching the affront, then struck the Sultan's shield with such a blow that the iron passed through it, striking him on his strongest plates of armor. The force of the encounter shook him so violently from his saddle that he rolled to the ground, tearing his helmet from his head. Thus Esplandian rode by gallantly, without having been touched. Queen Calafia and King Amadis rushed upon one another with pointed lances, both receiving blows on their shields in such a way that her spear broke into pieces, while Amadis' spear was thrown on the side. Then they both met shield to shield so forcefully that the Queen was thrown to the ground. Amadis' wounded horse also fell with his head injured, temporarily pinning Amadis beneath him. When Esplandian saw this he leaped from his horse and saved the King from further danger. Meanwhile the Queen, on the defensive, took her sword in hand and retreated with the Sultan, who rallied with great difficulty after his heavy fall, standing with his sword and helmet in hand. Although they attempted to fight very bravely, Esplandian, fortified by the presence of his beloved and valued princess, dealt such heavy blows with his superior military prowess and dexterity, that the bravest knight of the Pagans, the Sultan Radiaro, could neither give nor receive blows without constantly losing ground.

From Amadis de Gaule, Book 6, 1555 edition.

The Eminent Defeat

he Queen, joining the fight against Amadis, began attacking him with many fierce blows, some of which he received upon his shield, yet he dared not take up his sword. Instead he took a fragment of the broken lance which she had driven through his shield and struck her helmet, removing the crest ornament. When the Queen realized that he was only using the broken part of his lance to attack her, she queried him, "Why is this, Amadis? Do you consider my force so weak that you expect to conquer me with sticks?" To which he replied, "Queen, I have always been in the habit of serving women and aiding women, and since you are a woman, if I should employ weapons against you, I would deserve to lose all the honors I have ever earned." "What! You rank me just as a woman? You shall see now!" Taking her sword in both hands, she struck him with great rage. Amadis, still brave and strong, raised his shield to counter the blows, which cut it in half. Now, as they were close together, Amadis passed his stick into his left hand, seized her by the rim of her shield and pulled so forcibly that he broke the great thongs by which she grasped it. Taking it from the Queen and lifting it into the air, he forced her to kneel with one knee on the ground. When she quickly sprang up, Amadis tossed his own shield away, and seized the other one and the stick, and demanded of her, "Queen, yield yourself my prisoner, now that your Sultan has been conquered."

Woodcut illustration printed before 1501, in Der Bilderschmuck der Fruhdrucke.

The Surrender

She turned her head and saw that Esplandian had the Sultan already conquered as his prize. But she said, "Let me try one more time for the sake of fortune," and then raising her sword with both hands, she struck the crest of his helmet, hoping to cut it and his head in two parts. But Amadis warded the blow easily by turning away, striking her with the fragment of the lance upon the crest of her helmet so strongly that she was left dazed and stunned. As her sword fell from her hands, Amadis seized it and thus disarming her while catching her helmet so forcefully that he dragged it from her head, saying, "Now are you my prisoner?" She replied, "Yes, for there is nothing left for me to do." At this moment Esplandian approached them accompanied by the Sultan who had surrendered himself. With this conclusion, the Christian forces applauded the victory of King Amadis and Esplandian.

From Amadis de Gaule, Book 5, 1555 edition.

Sultan Radiaro and Queen Calafia are Ordered to be Taken to Princess Leonorina

In view of the entire army, they repaired to the royal encampment where they were received by all who applauded this military triumph. While this win was rather unremarkable in light of previous victories, it was a good omen for the future. King Amadis ordered Count Gandalin to lead the prisoners to Princess Leonorina, requesting that on behalf of himself and his son Esplandian that she honor the surrendered Sultan because he was such a great prince and strong noble knight. Furthermore, he implored that the Princess honor the captive Queen Calafia because she was a woman. He affirmed that he trusted in God that all future captives taken in battle should be forwarded to her encampment. Count Gandalin took charge of the prisoners and quickly delivered them to the palace in the city nearby.

From Amadis de Gaule, Book 9, 1548 edition.

Princess Leonorina Receives the Sultan and the Queen

Then arriving into the presence of the Princess, he delivered them to her with the message entrusted to him by Amadis, to which she replied, "Tell King Amadis that I thank him greatly for this present and I am certain that the good fortune and great courage of this adventure will happen again in pursuits that await us. We desire to see King Amadis here so when we discharge our obligation to his son, we may include him as a judge between us." The Count kissed her hand and returned to the royal camp. At this time the Princess sent her mother, the Empress, a request for a rich robe and matching headdress for the captive Queen to change into. She did the same for the Sultan, having sent for robes of her own father, the Emperor, after having their wounds dressed with certain preparations made by Master Helisbat. Then the Queen thought of her great fortune, and was amazed to see the great beauty of Leonorina. She said to her, "I tell you Infanta, that in the same way I was astonished to see the beauty of your cavalier Esplandian, I am equally overwhelmed beholding your loveliness. If your exploits and deeds correspond to the greatness of your appearance, I believe it is no dishonor to be your prisoner." "Queen Calafia", replied the Princess, "I hope the God in whom I trust will direct events so I shall be able to fulfill every obligation that conquerors should acknowledge toward their captives." The fighting continued and Kings Lisuate and Perion were killed. Finally the Pagans were routed, and the Emperor retired from the throne.

From Amadis de Gaule, Book 6, 1550 edition.

Esplandian and Leonorina Take the Throne of Constantinople from her Father, and They Wed

When Queen Calafia saw the nuptials of Esplandian and Leonorina, she relinquished all hope of uniting with him even though she loved him. For a while her courage waned as she appeared before the new Emperor Esplandian and the attendant lords. She addressed them, "I am a queen of a great kingdom abundant in worldly valuables such as gold and precious stones. My ancient lineage comes from royal blood dating back so far to a distant time of which there is no record of its start. My honor is as impeccable now as it was at my birth. My fortune has brought me to this distant land where instead of taking away captives as planned, I find myself a prisoner. Given all the great experiences of my life, both favorable and adverse, I believed I was strong enough to parry the whims of fortune in this recent battle. But my heart was tested and afflicted in my imprisonment because the beauty of this new emperor greatly overwhelmed me from the moment that my eyes looked upon him. I trusted with my fame and great fortune of my empire, that if I would convert to your religion, I might marry him myself."

French pre-1500, by the Master of the Roman de la Rose.

The Conversion of Queen Calafia

alafia continued, "When I came before this lovely Empress Leonorina I knew she and Esplandian should be joined, as they belonged together with their equal rank. That argument, which revealed the vanity of my thoughts, brought me to the conclusion which I now affirm. Since Eternal Fortune has taken the direction of my passion, I cast aside my own power because that outcome is not possible, and wonder, if it please you, if you think I should seek to marry some other man, perhaps a son of a king, with the powers of a good knight. And I will become a convert to the Christian faith. Seeing the organization of your religion and the great disorder of all others, I acknowledge that the law you follow must be the truth, while that which we follow is lies and falsehood."

From Amadis de Gaule, Book 6, 1555 edition.

A Wedding Arrangement is Negotiated

n hearing this, Emperor Esplandian embraced her with a smile and said, "Queen Calafia, my good friend, until now you have had neither word nor argument from me because I cannot permit myself to look on anyone without hatred, nor wish them well, unless they are bound by the holy law of truth. But now that the Omnipotent Lord has mercifully enlightened you to become his follower, you create in me a bond of love as if my father the King had fathered us both. As for your request for a husband, I will give you by my pledge a knight who surpasses the valor and lineage you have wished for." Then taking by the hand his cousin, Talanque, the son of the King of Sobradisa, a large handsome man, he said, "Queen, here you see one of my cousins, son of the King you see here, the brother of my father. Take him as your husband so that I may secure for you the good fortune which you will bring to this union." The Queen, impressed by his fine appearance, remarked, "I am satisfied with his presence, lineage and appearance, since you assure me of his merits. Please summon my sister Liota, who is with my fleet in the harbor, so that I may order her to station my forces." The Emperor sent Admiral Tartarie for her at once, who quickly brought her before the Emperor.

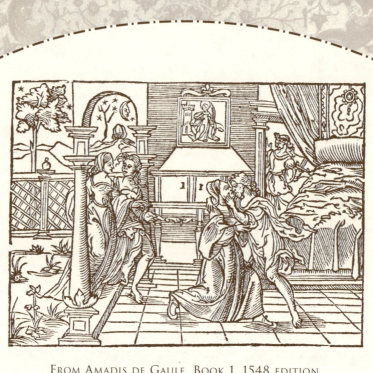

From Amadis de Gaule, Book 1, 1548 edition.

Liota Agrees to Calafia's Requests

xpressing her desires, Queen Calafia commanded and entreated Liota to agree to her wishes. Her sister Liota, kneeling upon the ground, kissed her hands and replied that the Queen need not explain her orders to those in her service. The Queen then raised her and embraced her, with tearful eyes, and led her by the hand to Talanque, saying, "Thou shall be my lord and the lord of my land, which is a very great kingdom. For your sake, this island shall change the custom which it has preserved for a very long time, so that generations of men and women shall succeed together henceforth, instead of the former order in which men have been separated. If you have a dear friend of the same rank as yours, let him be betrothed to my sister here, and in a short period of time, with your help, she shall be queen of a great land." Talanque greatly loved Maneli the Prudent, because they were brothers by birth and they held the same faith. He led him forward and said, "My Queen, since my lord the Emperor loves this knight as much as he loves me, and as much as I love thee, take him and guide his fate." Calafia replied, "Then I ask that we, accepting your religion, may become your wives."

From Amadis de Gaule, Book 5, 1555 edition.

The California Fleet Departs for Future Achievements

eeing that their wishes were confirmed, the Emperor Esplandian and the several Kings in attendance took Queen Calafia and her sister to the chapel, where they were converted to Christianity, and wed them to those two famous knights. They then converted all who were in their fleet. Immediately the order was given so that Talanque, commanding the well furnished fleet of his father Don Galaor, and Maneli heading the fleet of King Cildadan, should set sail with their new wives, plighting their faith to the new Emperor of Constantinople, pledging that if he should need any assistance from them, they would supply it as if for their own brother. Their future adventures and what happened to them subsequently I must be excused from telling in this tale, for they indeed endured many unusual circumstances with great valor in their chivalric quest to fight battles and gain kingdoms. But that story, if it would be related here, might present a certain jeopardy and therefore will not be told.

historical Chronology

1453   The Fall of Constantinople. The last Greek Emperor was Constantine.

1469   Marriage of Ferdinand of Aragon and Isabella of Castile.

1480   Spanish Inquisition began. Catholic rulers Ferdinand II and Isabella I promised freedom of religion for Muslims and Jews, but persecution and expulsion reigned.

1481   Christian Spanish campaign against Moors in Granada began.

1492   The Fall of Granada. Ferdinand II conquered the last Islamic enclave in Catholic Spain. Andalusia, the embodiment of Islamic culture in Spain ended.

1492   Columbus convinced Queen Isabella to sponsor his voyage of discovery to the New World.

1499   Granadan Muslims were given a choice of conversion or expulsion.

1508   First known printing of Garci Rodriguez de Montalvo's edition of the first four books of Amadis de Gaule in Zaragoza.

1510   First known printing of Montalvo's Book 5, Las Sergas de Esplandian in Seville.

1526   Peninsula later known as California was discovered by the Spanish.

1530s   Hernando Cortez led the exploration of the Pacific Ocean.

1540s   The name California was first noted in manuscripts and maps.

1542   After this date no edition of the Sergas de Esplandian was printed in Spain until 1575 and 1587, and then not again until 1857.

1544   First French translation of Esplandian by Herbaray des Essarts.

1862   Edward Everett Hale discovered an old copy of Esplandian in the Boston Library.

Further Reading

Hale, Edward Everett, THE QUEEN OF CALIFORNIA (Colt Press, 1945).

Herrin, Judith, A MEDIEVAL MISCELLANY (Viking Studio, 1999).

Innes, Hammond, THE CONQUISTADORS (Alfred A. Knopf, 1969).

Nicolle, David, Granada 1492, THE TWILIGHT OF MOORISH SPAIN (Osprey, 1998).

Menocal, Maria Rosa, THE ORNAMENT OF THE WORLD, HOW MUSLIMS, JEWS, AND CHRISTIANS CREATED A CULTURE OF TOLERANCE IN MEDIEVAL SPAIN (Little, Brown and Company, 2002).

Rodriguez de Montalvo, Garci , LAS SERGAS DE ESPLANDIAN (reprint of the 1587 edition by the Instituto de Cultura de Baja Califonia, Doce Calles, 1985).

Mijatovich, Chedomil, CONSTANTINE: THE LAST EMPEROR OF THE GREEKS — THE CONQUEST OF CONSTANTINOPLE BY THE TURKS (Samson Low, Marston & Co, 1892).

O'Connor, John, AMADIS DE GAULE AND ITS INFLUENCE ON ELIZABETHAN LITERATURE (Rutgers University Press, 1970).

Polk, Dora Beale, THE ISLAND OF CALIFORNIA, A HISTORY OF THE MYTH (University of Nebraska Press, 1991).

Runciman, Steven, THE FALL OF CONSTANTINOPLE 1493 (Cambridge University Press, 1969).

Southey, Robert, CHRONICLE OF THE CID (George Routledge & Sons, 1887).

Thomas, Hugh, RIVERS OF GOLD, THE RISE OF THE SPANISH EMPIRE, FROM COLUMBUS TO MAGELLAN (Random House, 2003).

TRANSACTIONS AND PROCEEDINGS OF THE GEOGRAPHICAL SOCIETY OF THE PACIFIC: THE ORIGIN AND MEANING OF THE NAME CALIFORNIA AND CALAFIA, THE QUEEN OF THE ISLAND OF CALIFORNIA (The Geographical Society of the Pacific, 1910).

Virgoe, Roger, editor, PRIVATE LIFE IN THE FIFTEENTH CENTURY (Weidenfelf & Nicolson, 1989).

Public Art Depicting Montalvo's Queen Calafia

- Murals containing Queen Calafia can be viewed in the Room of the Dons at the Intercontinental Mark Hopkins Hotel in San Francisco, California, created by Maynard Dixon and Frank von Slown in 1926.

- A large mural containing Calafia adorns the wall of the Senate Budget Committee Chambers in California's State Capital, Sacramento, created by Lucille Lloyd in 1936.

- The central panel of an incised limestone bas-relief on the exterior walls of the Library of the Coronado High School, San Diego, California, depicts Calafia and two Amazons, sculpted by Donal Hord in 1939.

- Queen Califa's Magical Circle, a sculpture garden of 9 large scale figures, includes a 15 foot tall figure of Califia's one eyed beast, is in Kit Carson Park, Escondido, California, sculpted by the French artist Niki De Saint Phalle in 2003.

- Whoopi Goldberg portrays Calafia, the narrator of the film GOLDEN DREAMS at Disney's California Adventure, Anaheim, California.